MIND

and

ME

SUNITA CHAWDHARY

KO
KNIGHTS OF

WOOOOOOOOA

CHAPTER ONE

AAAHHHHHHH!!!

Imagine waking up to *that!*

Well, believe it or not, that is exactly what I woke up to today.

It was very early (way too early to be up) and I was still very, *very* sleepy . . .

But *Mind* had other ideas. Mind was VERY keen to start the day.

And once Mind was up, there was no chance of getting back to sleep. Mind was already bustling about like a whirlwind of excitement, spinning all around. Mind swirled my way, tossing me up into the air like a pancake and out of bed.

I pressed my toes into the bobbly rug under my feet and wondered what on earth Mind was up to.

It was still dark outside. The rest of the house was quiet. No one else was up yet. Not even Pooey. She's usually the first one up.

Pooey always starts her day (and mine) by rustling around. She has to sleep in my room, so once she's up all I can hear is RUSTLE, RUSTLE, RUSTLE.

Strangely, this morning there wasn't a peep out of Pooey. In case you were

wondering, Pooey is my pet rabbit. Pooey sleeps in her little rabbit house, right next to my bed. Every day, I take her out to play and every night before I go to bed, I make sure she's all snug and tucked up in her bed of hay and sawdust.

SILLY SAMOSA

SOFT SAWDUST

CARROTY TREAT TOY (A TOY YOU CAN EAT!)

WIRY WINDOW

DRIPPY BUNNY BOTTLE

SCRUMPTIOUS SNACK

HAY FOR HUNGRY HARES

POOEY'S POO

So, if no one else was up yet (not even the sun!) what was up with Mind?! I flicked the light switch on and was shocked to find ... Pooey was *GONE!*

Well, that explained the louder-than-you-can-imagine: '*WOOOOooooooooooooO OOOOOOOAAAAAAAAAAAAHHHHHi!!!*'

Mind knew something was off, long before I'd realised anything was wrong.

The door on Pooey's hutch was wide open. I couldn't believe my eyes. How did Pooey open it all by herself?!

If that wasn't odd enough, Mind spotted something else…

A trail of rabbit poo!

It led all the way out of my room. But Pooey had never left my room on her own before. We *had* to investigate. We did the only thing we could.

We followed Pooey's poo!

We followed the teeny, tiny poos all the way out of my room.

Mind and I leapt through the air, over the trail of poo and across the landing. It was like

a strange dance on a dark and silent stage. The only light, peeking out at us through the gap in my bedroom door, shone bright like a spotlight. We crawled past my parent's room, quieter than a pair of spiders trying to get by without getting caught. Mind had to remind me about the creaky floorboards. We hopped over them to get to the moonlit staircase.

Pooey's poo had led us to the top of the stairs.

But Pooey had NEVER gone downstairs by herself before.

Something funny's going on. Something BAD. Mind was sure of it.

Mind was also certain that the last thing we needed was for everyone to find out Pooey was missing.

This was OUR mystery and we had to solve it all on OUR own.

So we crept down the stairs, trying not to make a sound.

We followed the trail into the kitchen, counting each and every little poo along the way ... 1, 2, 3, 4, 5 ... but before I knew it I'd lost count ...

and Mind had wandered off too!

Mind loves to explore. That means, *everything* can distract Mind. And when Mind's distracted, no matter how hard I try, we get *nothing* done. It wasn't long before we got distracted thinking about rabbit poo. The thing about rabbit poo is that each poo looks a bit like a chocolate chip . . .

Mmmmm . . . chocolate chip COOKIES!!! Mind's thoughts turned to food.

Uh oh. My tummy started to rumble.

GRRRRRRRRGGGGLLLLLLEEE

Shhhhh . . . whispered Mind.

But it was too late. Papa was awake. We heard his heavy footsteps creaking through the kitchen ceiling right above us. I knew it was Papa because it always sounded like giant frogs croaking when he came down the stairs. I heard Papa call out my name as he marched in, leaving the sound of frogs behind–

'Maya!'

Mind froze! I didn't know what to do.

Next thing I knew, Papa had switched on all the lights and he found me standing there – in the middle of the kitchen with rabbit poo everywhere.

'Maya, why are you up at this time of day?' he asked, blinking at the clock on the wall.

What was I supposed to say? I didn't want

to get told off for losing Pooey.

'And *why* is there rabbit poo everywhere?' he looked down at the floor.

Just then, Mind had a brilliant idea!

Why don't we make something up?

It made sense. Why tell Papa something he wouldn't want to hear, when we could tell him something he *would* want to hear?

So I told Papa a BIG, HORRID, OOPSY-DAISY (could this get more CRAZY?!) . . .

L I E ! ! !

'Errr . . . I was cleaning out Pooey's hutch!' I started with something he always wanted to hear.

Mind was speechless . . . so started trying to *show* me what to say next by acting out the words. But Mind just ended up looking like a poo-juggling, hula-hooping, whistle-blowing giraffe, as tall as the tale I was about to tell.

'I–I was taking the poo outside to throw it away . . . but then I fell down . . . and it slipped out of my hands.'

Papa sighed. For a moment, I thought he didn't believe me.

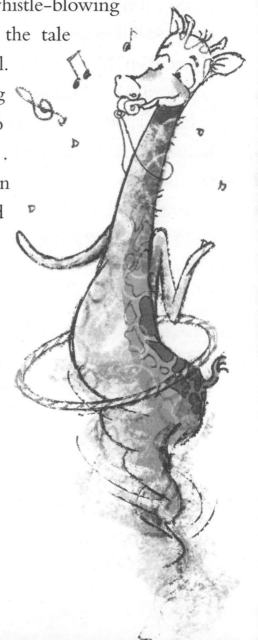

'Why didn't you ask for some help?'

I shrugged my shoulders and then I did something I never thought I would do . . . I lied AGAIN!

'I wanted to give you a surprise!'

'You silly billy,' he said with a smile that made the dimples in his cheeks dip in and out.

'You didn't need to do that!'

The *really* silly thing was that I had lied . . . not once, but TWICE.

That's asking for DOUBLE the TROUBLE! Mind warned me (a few hula-hoops too late).

We'd agreed to tell a lie. But not two of them!

Another creaky chorus over our heads made Mind and me look up. Except . . .

we knew there were no frogs upstairs, only floorboards. Oh no! That could only mean one thing . . .

We'd woken up Mama!

We could always tell when it was Mama because her footsteps were light and quick.

'Did you find Maya?' her sleepy words trickled down the stairs, through the hallway and into the kitchen, before she appeared through the doorway.

'Oh, yes, I sure did.' Papa reported back to her over his shoulder.

'Where was she?' Mama yawned, her eyes still not fully open as she shuffled forwards into the light.

'Kitchen *mey milli,*' Papa replied in *Hinglish.* That's what Mama and Papa call it when they speak to each other in a mix of Hindi and English. Hindi is another language we speak sometimes. Mama is from India, which makes me half Indian. Not that you can draw a line halfway down me through my belly button and say which half is Indian. Anyway, I like learning new words and it feels special when we speak in our very own made-up language Hinglish. It's like a secret code.

'*Frühstücken?*' Papa asked us if we wanted breakfast. Not in Hinglish this time, but German.

Papa used to work in Germany, so he likes to throw in a few words of German too! I don't know much German, so it's mostly Hinglish for me. But Mind loves putting languages together and hearing the different sounds merge into each other, like musical instruments in a group playing together making a new blended sound.

It made me think that when we spoke a mix of all three languages at home (Hindi and German and English) we should really call it: 'Hin-Ger-ish'.

Sounds like Ginger-ish! Mind chuckled. Funny because gingerish is exactly the way I would describe the colour of Pooey's fur coat. Which reminded me – we were looking for Pooey!

GRRRRRRRGGGLLE . . . My tummy started to rumble again.

'You must be hungry!' Papa patted my belly gently and squeezed me like a tube of toothpaste. I could hear the smile in Papa's voice. I turned around and saw it in his eyes. It would only disappoint him if

I told him about Pooey.

'Go brush your teeth and I'll make us something yummy for breakfast!' He grinned and swiped side to side, pretending to brush his teeth.

But the truth was, my appetite had disappeared.

I looked around with no idea where Mind had got to.

I started to feel like I was losing EVERYTHING – first Pooey, then my appetite, and now Mind!

I had been so busy worrying about Pooey that I forgot to check on Mind! I wondered if Mind was hungry too. There are times when Mind can seem like a mystery. But there are some things about Mind that are *very* predictable. If Mind is hungry or tired, (or worse, both hungry *and* tired at the same time) Mind is bound to be cranky. And *that* is when we get into a real *flap*. That's what Mind calls it when we're panicking.

I charged upstairs, wishing more than anything that Pooey would be in my room, waiting for me. Then everything would be normal again and no one would ever know I had lost Pooey, or that I had lied about it.

Wishing and hoping and imagining that Pooey was there, I pushed open the door to my room and found . . . pacing around and looking *very* worried . . . was . . . no, not Pooey (if only!) . . . a very unhappy Mind.

The BEST thing about Mind is that together we can *think* and *feel* and *do* ANYTHING.

But sometimes, that's also the WORST thing about Mind . . .

Mind could change like the weather. One minute, cold and grey. The next, warm and bright.

Right now, Mind was swelling up into a ginormous, angry, dark cloud overhead. Mind's arms were tightly crossed and face scrunched up into a miserable frown that gave off the *flappiest* vibes.

Yup. Mind was in a FLAP. That was the last thing we needed now, I thought, rolling my eyes. Then I took a deep breath and reminded myself – Mind was always there for me, no matter how *flappy* I got. So, I had to help Mind calm down.

'Cheer up, Mind!'

Sizzling, hot, little lightning bolts fired out of Mind. I was *not* about to get in the way of those. Bringing Mind back from the brink of a thunderstorm of worry was going to be tougher than usual.

'Chill out!' I yelled firmly. 'There's no need to be so upset.' I hoped Mind might hear me through the noisy howls of stormy winds building up.

But telling Mind not to feel something only made the feelings *worse*. After all, you can't control your feelings.

I usually knew how to take care of Mind. You could say it's a bit like having another pet. You might think that sounds like fun, but it isn't always that simple.

Mind can be fluffy and snuggly, or FIERCE and *ouchy!*

Mind can be LOUD and *scary*, or quiet and scaredy.

And, Mind can be all those things at once, which sounds impossible, doesn't it?!

If looking after Mind was just like taking care of a pet, that would be easy peasy. But Mind isn't like any one creature. When Mind is stressed, Mind is like ALL the animals you could ever imagine in one. And right now, *everything* about Mind reeked of STRESS!

Imagine training a wild dragon, totally out of control and ready to set fires with every

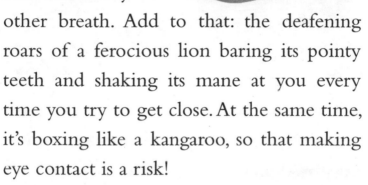

other breath. Add to that: the deafening roars of a ferocious lion baring its pointy teeth and shaking its mane at you every time you try to get close. At the same time, it's boxing like a kangaroo, so that making eye contact is a risk!

Dipping under Mind's fiery breath shooting my way and avoiding a punch to my chest, I lunged forwards to grab my socks off the floor, but Mind swooped in. It was like a pushy seagull, claiming its share of leftover greasy chips on the roadside and ready to fight off anyone who got in its way.

KAAAWWWW!

I was sure Mind didn't mean any harm, but it's hard to remember that when you're busy dodging fireballs. Mind *had* to cool off eventually and would probably end up feeling more like a SHEEPish dragon-lion-kangaroo-bird thing.

I needed to find out what was behind all the AGGRO. The only way to do that was to get Mind to open up.

'It's okay to feel upset,' I tried more

gently, in between flaps and roars.

Mind looked at me and paused, mid-fire-raging roar.

'Let's think this through,' I whispered. 'There's *always* a way out of the muddle.'

Mind's teeth-baring boxing came to halt. And, finally, Mind's furious feather flapping stopped.

Mind's scaly dragon's tail disappeared, and its frazzled feathers vanished one by one. I ran my fingers softly through Mind's mane as it fell out and faded away.

'Whenever I'm upset, you always help me feel better. I'm here for you.'

Mind erupted into a fountain of tears, rolling down like molten lava out of a volcano.

'We're a team!' I smiled.

Mind shrunk right down and slumped into a wobbly blob of jelly, looking up at me with sorry eyes.

Mind couldn't help but wonder: *How could we have let this happen?! Pooey has never escaped like this before. We've never kept a secret like this before.*

It felt like all the nevers were happening, all at the same time.

Mind was full of questions, but I had no answers.

Why did we lie to Papa? How are we going to get out of this mess?? What do we do now???

We would be in so much trouble if we couldn't find Pooey. It wasn't worth thinking about.

'No one else knows there is a problem . . . yet . . .' I reassured us both.

So let's fix it and quick, before anyone finds out! Mind spluttered.

We had no choice but to solve the mystery.

We had to go back downstairs and follow that trail of rabbit poo – that was the ONLY way to find Pooey.

First, I thought I'd better do as Papa had said. But Mind wouldn't let me brush my teeth in peace. Mind was hanging over me like a smelly fart that just wouldn't go away.

Then Mind started stomping and banging, like a fart parade following me around.

Part of me felt worried and impatient, like Mind . . .

After all, I had an empty belly, a guilty conscience *and* a MYSTERY to solve . . . The mystery of the missing Pooey!

But we had to be patient. It takes TIME to solve a mystery. The bigger the mystery, the longer it takes to solve . . . and this was by far our biggest mystery yet.

Suddenly I could smell something else . . .

Mmmmmmmmmmmm . . . PANCAKES . . . my faaavourite! The sides of Mind's mouth curled up with delight at the thought. Mind didn't need more than a whiff to recognise

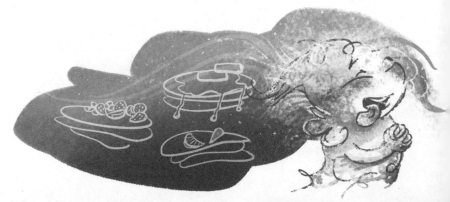

exactly what was cooking for breakfast all the way downstairs in the kitchen.

Mind can be brilliant at thinking. Sometimes s l o w a n d s t e a d y like a tortoise, deep in thought. At other times, Mind is full of *racing thoughts* that move faster than I can keep up with.

Come to think of it . . . Mind can be really *sharp,* especially first thing in the morning after a good night's rest and something to eat. And I don't mean sharp like pokey or prickly. I mean *sharp as a tack* – that's what Papa says about himself when he figures something out quicker than anyone else.

We needed our best thinking heads on if we were going to solve this mystery. I had to get Mind fed first. Top priority.

We tiptoed out of my room and made our way back downstairs. Mind wanted to slide down the bannister, so we wouldn't step on the precious poo trail. That's when I noticed, there was no rabbit poo on the stairs . . . In fact, there was no rabbit poo ANYWHERE!

I rushed downstairs and stumbled into the kitchen, where Papa was standing. To my horror, he was holding the dustpan and brush. He had swept away all the poo. There was no trail left to follow, and no trace of Pooey.

We'll never find Pooey now.

Pooey was lost . . . **FOREVER.**

CHAPTER 2

DING-DONG! The doorbell rang.

Mind wondered . . . *Could it be Pooey?*

If Pooey had opened her hutch door to escape, maybe she knew how to ring the doorbell too?!

My eyes lit up. Imagine if it *was* Pooey at the front door. I'd scoop her up in my arms and everything would be okay again.

I ran over and watched Mama open the door. Waiting outside on the front porch, was–

–Aunty Dolly (definitely *not* Pooey).

Silly Mind!

Of course Pooey couldn't hop high

enough to reach the doorbell.

The moment Aunty Dolly saw me, she sang my name out loud and clapped her hands, the way she always does:

♫ HI-YAAA MA-YAAA LA LA LA LA LA-LAAA ♪

She loved to make rhymes with my name: 'Hiya Maya!'; 'Maya's on fire!'; 'Maya's Empire'; all sorts of funny things to make me smile. Aunty Dolly was my *favourite* aunty. Everything she said sounded like a song. And every step she took looked like a dance. If anyone could cheer me up, it was Aunty Dolly.

She twirled around and gave me a hug. 'Do-wap do-wap dee-doo – and how do *you* do?'

I couldn't help but hug her even tighter. Mind was busy thinking about other things.

Aunty Dolly had her yellow yoga mat

with her. I'd been so busy trying to solve the mystery that I'd forgot it was yoga day. Every Saturday, Mama had Aunty Dolly over for yoga. I never joined in because Mind never kept still long enough for me to!

Right behind Aunty Dolly, were my cousins: Tanya and Anya.

Tanya and Anya are *identical twins*. That means they look *exactly* like each other but it doesn't mean they *are* like each other.

In fact, anyone who knows them can always tell them apart, because they're so different in every other way.

Tanya is really LOUD and Anya is really *quiet*. Tanya likes to be funny and Anya is usually serious. Tanya wears multi-coloured tutus (she says that's because she's a rainbow unicorn fairy) but Anya prefers more ordinary looks that she calls *sensible*.

The BIGGEST difference between them is that Tanya *hates* animals, while Anya *loves* them. And that means they both always ask me exactly the SAME question whenever they visit:

'WHERE IS POOEY???'

I knew that was the *first* thing they were going to ask me, but it was the *last* thing I wanted anyone to ask right now!

Mind had a plan . . . If we distracted them, maybe they wouldn't ask about you-know-who!

Tanya tap-danced in, waving her arms in the air musically. Anya followed her, not dancing or waving. She hopped in slowly, a bit like a shy rabbit.

Anya looked around. Her nose twitched. She looked up towards my room. I knew what was coming . . .

She looked at me curiously and asked, 'Where is P– '

'HEY!' I cried, before Anya could finish her question. 'Let's all play Dizzy Dodge'ems!'

I started spinning.

'Yayyyyyyyyy!!!' Tanya joined in.

Soon, Anya was spinning on the spot too, and then Mind. We went around and around.

I was just starting to get dizzy when I heard–

'Girls!'

The sound of Mama's voice stopped me.

Mind kept going, spinning around me.

Wheeeeeeeeeeeeeeeeeee!

Before we knew it, we were all bumping into each other and falling over.

'Right. Enough!' Mama sounded cross.

Mama's voice always changed a bit when other people were around.

'Excuse me, everyone! Pooey's poo coming throoough!' Papa squeezed past, carrying out the bins.

No one took much notice as he weaved his way between us. Only *I* knew that Papa was walking off with bags full of precious poo he'd chucked away, and with it the all-important poo trail that could've led us to Pooey.

At least Papa taking the bins out would cheer Mama up. It also meant that it was Mama's turn to do the dishes. She says that washing up is the closest she gets to a bubble bath these days. She even has a special dish-washing ritual.

First, she carefully placed her super soft mat under the kitchen sink, poised to squish her feet into. Next, she slipped on her favourite pair of neon blue rubber gloves. Finally, she turned the squeaky taps to fill the sink and hoisted the bottle of washing-up liquid as high as her arm could reach before pouring it in.

It drizzled down like cool golden syrup melting onto warm buttery pancakes. As the sink brimmed with soapy white water and bubbles, her face broke into a relaxed smile. From where I was standing, I could see the tiniest of bubbles rising up like rainbow-coloured thoughts floating freely out of her head.

Nothing could spoil her moment of bliss. And I wasn't about to burst her happy bubbles by telling her what was really going on.

I scanned the room for Mind, who was honing in on Papa. Usually, watching Papa move through the obstacle course of the cluttered narrow washroom was like watching a not-so-graceful gymnast. His goal was to balance the bin bags delicately enough to not snag them on anything. Papa hoicked the clothes drying rack with his elbow so it snapped shut, then turned sideways on one foot and twisted around to click the washing machine door into place with the heel of his other foot, making room to shuffle by. Mind was mesmerised by Papa's new moves.

Leaning forward, Papa pushed the handle of the back door down with his chin. He curled his toes and used the edge of his slipper to yank open the door. At the last second he swung his head back, making way for the door as it purred open.

Papa stepped out into the garden, his slippers slapping against the soles of his feet clumsily as he hummed out of tune.

The path he had cleared led to a bright day outside. And *that* was the escape Mind was looking for.

Quick! Let's go!

Mind was desperate to keep Tanya and Anya away from my room. The back garden looked like the best way out – out of the house and out of the dilemma we were in.

Suddenly, something orange and fuzzy launched itself across the garden. *Pooey?!*

Mind bounded over for a closer look. But it was just the neighbour's marmalade tabby cat sitting in the long grass. She sprung up again and clapped her paws, trying to catch a butterfly. But it flitted away in circles without a care and disappeared.

'Mmmmmmmmmmm! Look at these YUMMY pancakes!' Aunty Dolly lured us back into the kitchen.

She took the pan off the stove where Papa had left it and flipped the pancakes one at a time, into a wonky pile on a plate. The smell of fresh pancakes wafted by. Mind sprinted

over like a hungry pup, slobbering tongue hanging out and wagging tail following behind. I shook my head sternly at Mind.

'There's *no* time to waste! We have to check on Tanya and Anya – what's to say they aren't already on their way up the stairs and about to discover Pooey is missing?!'

Mind scowled.

Mind wasn't about to do *anything* for *anyone* on an empty stomach. So, I quickly grabbed a couple of pancakes to take along with us.

'More for *meee!*' Aunty Dolly shrugged, taking a seat at the table and tucking in.

Mind followed me faithfully back to the hallway, if only to snatch the pancakes from my grip. In one of the biggest bites I've ever witnessed, Mind gobbled both pancakes at once, like a delicious pancake burger.

NOM!
NOM!
NOM!

'Hey! Those were meant for both of us to *share!*' I huffed.

Mind was too busy licking sticky syrupy fingers to pay any attention, leaving me wishing I'd had at least a taste of a pancake.

But THIS was our chance. The grown-ups were all out of our way. They wouldn't be for long. We *had* to be quick.

I pulled Mind along by the hand. We sped down the corridor but there was no sign of Tanya or Anya.

Thankfully, right at the bottom of the staircase, we found Tanya perched on the edge of the last step. She was restless, tapping her foot on the wooden floor.

'Where's Anya?!' my eyes darted around.

'She went to the loo.' Tanya grumbled.

'Upstairs or downstairs?!'

Mind panicked and scooted up the stairs to check.

'She's right *there*,' Tanya pointed behind me, where Anya had just popped out of the toilet.

I heard Mind jogging into my room and back to the landing again. Mind peered down at us and let out a sigh of relief like a whoopee cushion, floating all the way down into a deflated heap on the floor.

I stepped over Mind,

tired of the antics. One of us had to stay focused if we were going to find Pooey, and it was becoming clear to me that I'd have to lead the way. I had really hoped that feeding Mind would bring out the smart, problem-solving Mind I knew was somewhere in there. Maybe it was all getting to be too much for Mind.

'Follow me, everyone!' I decided to try a different approach.

I led them towards the kitchen, Mind prancing playfully behind me, and then into the washroom in a series of leaps and jumps. Tanya and Anya followed curiously. But just before we got to the back garden, they stopped. We were *so* close!

'Where *are* we going, Mayaaa?' Tanya whined.

Anya reached into her pocket for her phone. In that moment I knew it was MAKE or BREAK. If Anya got her phone out, it was all OVER. We would *never* convince either of them to come outside to play.

'WAIT!' I shouted so loudly that even Aunty Dolly had to look up from the kitchen table, mid-crossword puzzle. A couple of pigeons fluttered away outside.

TRAMPOLINE TIME!

Miraculously, Mind's memory kicked in! Papa had set up the trampoline in the garden last night, ready for us to use today. *That* was the stroke of pancake-fuelled genius we needed!

'Whoever gets to the trampoline first . . . WINS!'

Everyone knew that Tanya couldn't resist a challenge. She always had to be the winner. And, whenever they visited, Tanya and Anya always wanted a go on Papa's famous hand-built trampoline.

Tanya's eyes twinkled at the possibility of winning.

'Ready! Set! GO!' she squawked, pushing past Mind and me.

'Wait for me!' Anya squeaked, hands out of her pockets and into fists fit for running.

CHAPTER 3

BOING! BOINGG!! BOINGGG!!!

Tanya was bouncing up and down on the trampoline, showing off her most impressive routine yet. Star jumps! Back flips!! The WORKS!!! With every jump she threw her arms higher and higher up in the air. Her pigtails reminded me of Pooey's flippity-floppity bunny ears when she hopped around.

'Come up here!' Tanya called out to us. 'It's like being on top of the world!'

I didn't feel like being on top of the world. But Mind insisted we join in and gave me a leg up.

Mind's point of view was:

There's NO POINT feeling sorry for ourselves. It is the weekend after all!

But, when I looked down all I could see were yellow dandelions popping up at us, as if to say: *Where's Pooey today?* (Dandelion leaves were Pooey's *favourite* garden treat).

'Yaaaaaaaaayyyyyy!!!' Tanya dived into the trampoline on her belly, then bounced on her bottom and threw herself into a high jump, like she was playing a giant drum. The whole surface wobbled and flung us up one by one. Pooey's playpen lay empty and I couldn't stop staring at it.

WOOOOOOOO-HOOOOOOOOOO!

Mind didn't seem to share my guilty feeling. So I closed my eyes and tried to shake it off. Tanya stopped for Anya to get on. The trampoline settled into a gentle rocking that felt calming.

I looked up and spotted a single, small cloud. It swept slowly by and started to change shape.

Loooook! A friendly snail, with a round shell and cute little antennae.

Mind's eyes closed lazily.

'Here we gooooooooooo!!!'

It felt like Tanya was trying to beat the highest of high jumps and set a new trampoline World Record, jolting Mind back to reality with a BOOM!

My eyes blinked open, and the snail cloud transformed into . . . a RABBIT, lost and lonely, surrounded by *endless* sky.

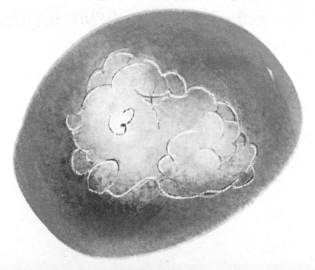

Mind gasped, suddenly remembering: *POOEY!*

A pigeon patrolling the garden fence cooed at Mind. That got Mind thinking . . .

. . . Pooey couldn't have gone far, the fence went all the way around the garden.

I wasn't so sure that meant Pooey was safe.

The neighbour's cat pounced at a squirrel scurrying out of the grass and over the fence. That was enough to worry me about all the scary things out there that Pooey had never faced alone before. Just *imagine* Pooey up against that cat with its claws . . . Pooey had NO chance.

I felt awful. I'd do ANYTHING to get Pooey back home and safe.

Mind, on the other hand, wanted to do anything to make me feel better. Mind couldn't bear to see me like this. Mind knew that until I felt better, neither of us would be able to enjoy ourselves.

Anya tapped my shoulder.

'Are you OK, Maya? You seem blue.'

At first, I wondered what she meant.

Blue? Mind turned my hands around to check my nails. Then Mind yanked down my lower eyelids to examine my eyes. I wasn't *turning* blue (to Mind's relief). So what did Anya mean?

Maybe she meant blue like the rain. It was like a miserable rainy day inside me, even though outside the sun was shining brightly.

It was a *sad* feeling. Mind just SIGHED. No *are you okay?* No cuddles. Nothing.

Well, wallowing isn't exactly how we planned to spend the weekend . . .

'Fair point, but we didn't exactly *plan* for Pooey to go missing!'

Mind *hates* it when there is a problem we can't figure out. I just couldn't see a way forward. I felt STUCK in a box with no way in or out of its four sides. So Mind found a *clever* and *creative* way to STEP IN and get me OUT!

Holding me up by my ankles, Mind thrust me into the big BLUE sky. It felt like we were flying in a rocket ship, flaring through the Earth's atmosphere and into space!

If only we could look down at ourselves from that distance . . .

Look! Listen! FEEL the MAGIC of the blue-ness all around you!

BLUE is the colour of sunny skies above and waves in the seas below. The whole world and all its wonders . . . the blue planet!

BLUE! The colour of our blue gods that keep us safe.

BLUE! The colour of LIFE!

Gliding back down to Earth, we hovered over leafy treetops. Mind tipped a watering can and sprinkled glittery *blue* droplets over all the flowers and fruits.

The wind blew my hair up over my eyes and ears. We landed back on our feet, exactly where we were standing before. But *here* and *now*, we were back with a new take on things.

Mind made some pretty good points. And managed to cheer me up (a bit) too. It was enough to get us back on track!

We had to *believe* it was possible before we could get anywhere.

If we stop believing that we can find Pooey, then we might as well give up now.

In our heads and in our hearts, we had to stay POSITIVE.

We jumped off the trampoline together, not wasting another moment.

'We have to get on with it. We still have a mystery to solve.'

Now, with no poo to follow . . .

Imagining ourselves flying had given me an IDEA!

'Maybe looking for Pooey on the ground isn't the only way . . . Where's the *highest* point we can get the BEST view of the garden from?'

Mind blinked a couple of small white petals away. A few more danced over to us. I brushed them out of Mind's hair. Where were they coming from? I followed them up with my eyes . . . They were twirling off the trees in the breeze.

Another petal landed on Mind's nose. **AHH . . . AAHHH . . . AAH-CHHHOooO!!!**
Mind looked perplexed. But, it couldn't be clearer to me. We had to get *above* the ground to get the best view.

We couldn't really get to outer space and we didn't need to go quite that far.

So how
could we
get higher
up in the
garden…?

'The TREE house!'

Of course!

Mind wiped away the snotty
sneeze and cartwheeled towards the
tree house.

'Wait for me, Maya!' Anya
skipped over, catching me by
surprise. 'Are you OK?'

Maybe, just *maybe*, I thought,
Anya and Tanya would be
able to help. Part of me

wanted to tell them *everything*. But I could only do that if Mind agreed. We always stuck together. Mind always had my back and I wasn't about to go behind Mind's back.

I figured I could test the water with Anya. She was less likely to make me feel bad about it than Tanya.

'I've lost something . . .' I whispered in Anya's ear.

But Mind overheard from about three cartwheels away and stopped to glare at me. I hadn't meant to upset Mind! I didn't think Mind would, well . . . *mind!*

'You've *lost* something?!' Tanya shrieked as if she'd won a prize.

I couldn't believe Tanya had heard me too. She was so OVER THE TOP and unpredictable.

Mind was SEETHING.

Try getting us OUT of trouble, not into it!

'No one else was supposed to hear!' I tried explaining myself.

But Mind wasn't convinced.

'AHOY mateys!' Tanya barged in again, this time with a gruff, pirate voice.

'So yer lookin' for some hidden *treasure* across these choppy waters?'

She waved a hand past our faces in slow motion and gazed into the distance, as if at a wide open seafront.

'Aye, aye, Cap'n!' Anya saluted her.

As far as Mind was concerned, I'd nearly let slip that we'd lost Pooey. Mind wasn't going to risk that happening again. So Mind shushed me with a look that would shush anyone with any sense. If that wasn't clear enough –

ZZZZZZZZZZIP! Mind zipped my mouth shut.

'So it's a *secret*, eh? Tanya winked and

poked me with a bony elbow. 'Sounds like the beginnin's of a TREASURE HUNT!'

'Arrrrr!' Anya growled.

I didn't think keeping it secret was the best way to find Pooey . . . but I had my doubts about telling anyone, especially the GROWN-UPS. Mind probably knew best.

We had to get to the tree house to look for Pooey.

'To the *ship*, me hearties!' I pointed to the tree house, playing along.

'ARRRRR!!!!' Tanya raced Anya there and Mind followed them, leaving me behind.

I looked back at the house and saw Mama through the window. She was still gloved up at the kitchen sink and smiling dreamily. Who knew how long we had left before they realised Pooey was gone? We had to hurry!

'ALL hands on deck!' Tanya yelled, from

the top rung of the fraying rope ladder.

Last to get there, I clambered aboard as fast as I could. Surely we would be able to spot Pooey in the garden from up here!

As soon as I got up, I was nearly knocked down by Tanya. She lifted an old knitted quilt crumpled in the corner and shook it open.

'Here! CATCH!' she threw one side of the fabric my way, while keeping a tight hold onto hers.

It felt rougher than I expected and was as FILTHY as it looked.

'Let's put it up, across

here, like this!'

She held up the quilt to show us how it would cover the open side of the tree house where the slide was.

Dragging my wooden toy box across the floor, bump-ity bumping along the gaps between the wooden panels, I almost lost my grasp on the quilt. Tanya stood on the box and secured the quilt to the wall, making it dark inside. She took a step back and smiled proudly.

A *gust* of wind WHOOSHED in . . . Suddenly the SHIP came to life! Sunshine burst in, lighting up bits of dust and wool off the quilt, like tiny fairies that hung around just for a magical moment and then vanished again.

With Captain Tanya at the helm, it didn't feel like we were standing next to a dirty quilt flapping in and out of our faces.

It was like the giant sail of a ship catching the wind and propelling us through wild waters!

Captain Tanya stood tall with her head held high and her hands on her hips.

'Now, all this mighty ship *needs* is a FLAG!'

Pffffffff! Mind blew a cobweb off an abandoned curtain rail leaning against the wall and passed the pole to me.

Tanya snatched it and pushed one end as hard as she could into a gap in the floor.

'Help me raise this mast, me hearties!' she grunted.

All together, we managed to squeeze the pole through and stand it upright in the middle of the treehouse. It was taller than any of us – almost as tall as the ceiling!

Ready to set sail!

Mind could see it all . . .

The mast of the ship stood tall above us, sails flapping overhead, flag flying high!

Tanya had a way of capturing everyone's attention that was *very* EXCITING . . . *so* exciting that we'd FORGOTTEN all about our plan to search for Pooey from the tree house!!

We had to get back on the case. I edged over to the window and beckoned Mind over quietly.

'*PSSSST* . . .'

We needed Tanya and Anya to keep playing while we concentrated on our MISSION.

I glanced over and noticed Tanya scratching her head as she came up with her next move.

'Shoes OFF, everyone!' she ordered.

What an *odd* thing to say – even for Tanya, who wasn't afraid of saying anything! Mind couldn't wait to see what she had in store for us.

But I pretended not to hear her and kept going. I tried to wedge open the window shutters with my fingernails. ERGHHH. They were jammed shut. I tried again, only to get pricked by a sharp splinter in my fingertip. Ouch! I pinched it out and squeezed my finger.

'I could use some help over here, Mind!'

But Mind was too busy following *Tanya's* instructions! Mind had taken off both shoes and was eye-balling mine. The CHEEK of it! Why wasn't Mind over *here* helping *me* instead of doing whatever Tanya said?

With two quick kicks, Tanya popped her shoes off, one of them landing right on Anya's bottom as she bent forwards to untie her shoelaces.

'Hey! Stop it!' Anya cried, turning to

check the back of her trousers. She patted away a footprint the shoe had made, then rubbed her bottom as if it was sore.

While those two got into a squabble, *I* got into the perfect position to shove open the window shutters. And that's when I felt something tugging at my left foot . . .

I couldn't believe it. It was *Mind* trying to pull my shoe OFF!!!

'What are you up to?!' I snapped.

Mind let go of my shoe and it dropped to the floor.

'Give me back my shoe, RIGHT NOW!'
I was *fuming*.

Mind shrivelled up into a crinkly mess on the floor and looked up at me, then down at the floor, eyes welling up with tears.

I'd lost my temper and felt bad for taking it out on Mind.

'Sorry for shouting, but I hurt my finger trying to open this window all by myself and you're not even paying attention. And now you're making me trip up.'

If that was my attempt at an apology, Mind was not impressed. *Hmph*.

My little finger throbbed and I wiggled my hand around to get rid of the pain. For such a small splinter, it really stung!

'AH-HAAAH!' Tanya exclaimed.

She leapt forward, making me flinch. She clasped my left foot between her hands like a crab's pincers.

'You're the *only* one wearing white socks, Maya!'

She rolled the sock off my foot then threw open the lid of the toy box. She fished around inside until she found a marker pen and started scribbling all over my sock.

I raised my eyebrows at Mind. 'Because of *you* messing around, Tanya's destroying my sock right now!'

Mind melted into a sulky puddle of SLIME.

I'd told Mind off again, even though I knew it wasn't all Mind's fault.

Mind slid away through the cracks in the tree house floor, leaving only a mucky patch of *sludge* behind. I guess Mind truly felt like rubbish and wanted to make sure I knew.

I went to get a closer look at my sock that

Tanya was setting on top of the mast. She'd drawn a smiley skull and written PIRATE SHIP on the other side.

'That's a useless flag. You can barely see it.' It wasn't like Anya to say something like that.

I guess she was still upset about the bum-shoe-kick incident.

Tanya gave her a moody HUMPH!

They obviously had unfinished business to quarrel over. So I left them to it. *I* had my *own* (more important) unfinished business.

I turned around and there was Mind again! Casually leaning out of the window, enjoying an imaginary sea view . . . I had no clue how Mind had got the shutters open. Maybe *melty* Mind had got into the hinges and managed to slick them open.

I scooped my binoculars out of the toy box and started inspecting the garden. There was grass . . . and grass . . . more grass . . . and then . . . some *more* grass. Sure, there were weeds, daisies, buttercups, dandelions, leaves, the odd bug here and there . . . but mostly just GRASS. The grass was so long that it wasn't very easy to see much else from up here. Even with my binoculars.

The sock-flag fell off the mast, onto my shoulder and then the floor. I took my binoculars off and looked at my poor sock lying there, covered in pen marks. No one cared if I minded Tanya taking my things and ruining my sock. Mind didn't seem to mind anything anymore. Mind was acting like Tanya's treasure hunt adventure was the most important thing in the world and was hardly interested in anything I was doing or thinking or feeling. It probably wasn't much fun being around *Miserable Maya*.

For Mind, it was far more tempting to feel good. And the best way to do that was to *ignore* anything bad . . .

Even if that meant ignoring the fact that WE STILL HADN'T FOUND POOEY!

CHAPTER 4

'Let me lookit me map!' grumbled Captain Tanya, of the Smiley Skull Pirate Ship.

'Are ya seein' this, me hearty?' she put her arm around me and hovered her pinky finger over an invisible map.

I wondered where she was going with this.

'Looks like we'll have to sail the Seven Seas to find this treasure,' she rolled her map up and swiftly pointed it out of the window of the tree house, almost taking my nose off with her hand.

'Let *me* see too!' Anya's head popped up between us, promptly followed by Mind.

Rolling my eyes in despair, I tilted my head away. I didn't get why everyone was acting as if this was such a big deal. Didn't they realise . . . there was NO MAP?!

'I don't think we're going to find the treasure this way,' I moaned.

'Avast! We have a TRAITOR aboard!' Tanya tugged me by the strap of my dungarees, towards the top of the slide. 'Ye'll walk the plank!'

'That's not fair!' Anya argued back. 'Maya's *not* a traitor!'

At least *someone* was still on my side.

'Mutinyyyyy!!!' Tanya squealed, crossing her arms and turning her nose up. 'That's what this is!'

'It's not a mutiny – you're still our Cap'n. But stop being so . . . *pushy!*'

She let go of me. I looked out of the window again. There had to be *some* kind of clue as to which way Pooey had gone.

What's THAT?!

Hundreds of bits of *something*, coppery in colour and feathery light, were drifting by. What were they? They weren't petals or leaves this time. Could it be . . . Pooey's FUR?!

Mama was standing on the patio holding a tray full of roasted peanuts. She rolled the roasted nuts on the tray over and over, until the skins came loose. Then with a flick of her wrists, she tossed them up and blew the skins away like she was blowing candles out on a birthday cake. Skinless peanuts rattled back into the tray. The skins lightly flew away down the garden and got caught in the apple trees. So the bits we had seen were just the peanut skins she was sifting out.

Ohhh sooo cool! Never seen anyone take peanut skins off like that before!

'It *is* cool, but it *isn't* a clue to finding Pooey.'

Or IS it . . . ? Mind looked at me as though I'd missed something obvious.

Mind grew two rabbit ears, one floppier than the other, just like Pooey's. Then, with quivering nose and whiskers,

73

Mind squatted on the floor and brought one foot all the way up behind a bunny ear, to do a leg scratch just like Pooey would. Fur moulted off, as Mind hopped out of rabbit mode and the hairs scattered around.

Next, Mind turned me into a detective, plonking an inspector's hat on my head and holding a magnifying glass to my face. Mind threw some of the hair out of the window, and we watched it fly away in a squiggly line, in the same direction of the peanut skins blowing in the wind.

According to Mind, if we wanted to find Pooey, all we had to do was look for gingerish fur!

'Sooo . . . we're looking for any fur that Pooey might have shed?' I tried to make sense of what Mind was saying.

Mind nodded smugly, as if *this* plan GUARANTEED finding Pooey.

'Then we need to get much *closer* to the ground.'

It sounded a bit OUT THERE to me. But at least Mind was back in the *game* (and not Tanya's pirate game!). Mind was trying to come up with helpful suggestions. It was better than anything I could think of right now, so had to be worth a try.

If nothing else, we might find out if Pooey had been in the garden AT ALL since going missing, which I was starting to question.

'Tharrr she BLOWS!!' Tanya honked in my ear.

'I see you've located treasure!' She looked out of the window where I'd been pointing. 'Found JEWELS in them apple trees, eh?!'

'Ooooooh!' Anya chimed in.

'Land ahoy! DOCK the SHIP!' Tanya swept the quilt off the wall.

'Hold yer horses! We're gonna need these

reigns to ride em, pardners!' She switched from Pirates at Sea, to Cowgirls of the Wild West, passing us a skipping rope each from the toy box.

'FOLLOW MEEE!' she swished down the slide.

'Wheeeee!' Anya followed her.

Heading over to the apple trees was *just* what we had in mind. That was the direction the wind, and any rabbit fur blowing in it, were going.

We could let Tanya and Anya speed on ahead while we came up with a strategy. That way, we could make sure we checked the garden properly and didn't miss any signs of Pooey's fur along the way.

'Let Tanya think she's in charge of – '

But without waiting for me to finish, Mind ZOOMED past!

Tanya made a loud NEIGHHHHHH

sound, grabbed her reigns and galloped off with Anya.

'YEEE-HAWWWW!!!' Mind followed.

I tried to get down, but lost my footing and nearly fell off! Mind didn't even stop to ask if I was okay.

I was full of *worry* but Mind was in such a *hurry* . . . It was almost as if it didn't matter how *I* felt. First, Mind was ignoring the problem, and now, Mind was ignoring *me!*

Mind wanted to keep playing pretend (pretending that nothing was wrong!), but Mind was only making things worse by taking off like that.

I lagged behind and took my time to scope out this end of the garden first, looking for any gingery fur I could find. I felt let down. Mind had left me with the toughest task: trawling for tufts of fur! And doing it alone was harder than I'd thought.

There were thousands, maybe *millions*, of blades of grass – never-ending stripes in different shades of green, some lit up and some in shadow. After a while of focusing on the lines, searching up and down, side to side, round and around, my eyes began to feel FUNNY. I looked away and gave them a rub.

Mama saw me and waved, wiggling her fingers in the air, before going back into the house.

If *only* it was someone else's fault and she could hear the news without *me* having to tell her myself . . .

Then I imagined something *even* WORSE than telling Mama myself. What if she went inside and switched on the actual news, to the horrific headline:

BREAKING NEWS!
*Beloved Bunny Binned
in Botched Burglary!!!*

What if Pooey had been STOLEN?! What if the burglars changed their minds when she started pooping all over the place?! What if they'd dumped her somewhere on their way to their next target?!

That *would* be breaking news . . . HEART-BREAKING! Mama's weekend would be spoilt. And it was the only break she got after her looooonnnnnggggg week at work. That's what she told Papa when they talked in the kitchen, downstairs at night

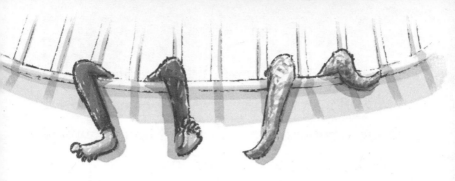

with the doors closed, thinking I couldn't hear them. Mind and I would sit out of sight upstairs on the landing, our legs dangling down between the stair railings.

We'd listen in to EVERYTHING they said. It was the ONLY way to know what was *really* going on. Grown-ups seem to think that children can't handle the truth. But what's worse is NOT knowing! *That's* what worries me more.

Like not knowing why I don't have a brother or sister like my friends do. I used to wonder about that all the time. I only found out because I overheard Mama and Papa talking about it one day, when they decided to get me a pet rabbit instead. If you asked *me* (not that anyone did), having Pooey was better than a brother or sister, because babies don't have whiskers that tickle you when you have cuddles, or soft paws for you to stroke when you snuggle up together on the sofa. Pooey was the best buddy I could've ever wished for.

Not knowing meant there was a gap left where the truth was supposed to be . . . a deep, dark and empty hole for lots of WORRIES to fill instead! Then out of nowhere, they'd jump out at you . . . Like, what *really* happened to Pooey? Probably not a 'botched burglary'. But *who knew???*

Everyone needs to know the truth, *especially* children.

Then I remembered, *I* was the one who hadn't told Papa the truth *today*. First thing this morning, when he asked me why I was up so early, I pretended everything was fine when it wasn't. I couldn't really complain about being kept in the dark about the things that grown-ups didn't want to tell *me* then, could I?

'Egh!'

I turned around. It was the neighbour's cat again. She'd been loitering by the bushes, licking herself the whole time I'd been looking for rabbit fur.

But *now*, she was up on all fours, hunching her back *really* WEIRDLY.

'Egh-Errrghhh . . . !'"

I had no idea what she was doing but I'd never seen anything so BIZARRE in my life.

'EGH . . . HEEEERRRRGH!!'

She coughed up a yucky hairball.

It rolled into the grass, bits of hair breaking off and leaving a trail of . . . GINGERISH FUR. It looked exactly like the fur I'd been searching for but hadn't found (until now). Well, that was the end of *that* plan. Even if there *was* gingery fur in the garden, there was no way of knowing if it belonged to

Pooey or if it was cat fur. I thought I'd better catch up with Mind and share the 'breaking' bad news.

CHAPTER 5

I'd decided: enough was enough. Pooey was *my* pet rabbit and it was *my* job to keep her safe. So I couldn't let anything or anyone get in the way of that. Not even Mind. If I needed to let someone in on the secret to help us find Pooey, then so be it.

'Right, everybody!' I announced my arrival at the apple trees.

But, Tanya was hanging like a monkey from a knobbly branch. Anya was trying to make a daisy chain. And Mind, was dozing under the shade of the tree.

We'd had an early start to our day but this was ridiculous. Snoozing while

Pooey was missing!

'Narrm!' Tanya plucked an apple and crunched into it.

Anya looked frustrated with a stem of a daisy that kept bending and wouldn't slot through the other like it was supposed to.

No one was bothered about me falling behind, or the fact that I'd finally made it over and had something to say.

'AAAAARRRRRGGGGGHHHHHHH!!!!!'

Tanya let out the shrillest cry *ever* and fell OUT of the tree.

Mind jumped up. Anya stopped threading daisies.

Tanya hopped up and down like she was on a flaming hot barbecue grill.

'UGGGGGHHHH!!' she screeched again like a siren.

'What's wrong?!' Anya asked, wide eyed.

'There's a WORM in that apple!!!'

Tanya whinged.

'Is that all?!' Anya snarled at Tanya's reaction.

'It's wiggling around right where I was about to take another bite!' Tanya winced, wiping her tongue with her sleeve.

'It's not a worm, it's a caterpillar. And *it* should be the one screaming,' Anya smirked. She knelt down and let it climb onto her finger.

'Ewww GROSS!'

'Don't listen to *her*,' Anya talked to the caterpillar in a baby voice and put it back on a leaf on the tree. 'You'll be a big beautiful butterfly one day. Then you can get away from anyone who tries to eat you.'

'I wasn't *trying* to eat it. That's disgusting!' Tanya wretched.

'Well, actually, bugs are full of protein, so they're not *disgusting* at all.' Anya used her nature know-how to outsmart Tanya.

'In *that* case, how about those EGGS in that bird's nest?! Eggs are full of protein too and YUMMIER!' Tanya gibed.

'Don't you dare! They're her babies!' Anya defended the mother bird who was whistling while watching over her nest.

THUD! An apple fell off the tree, onto the ground and knocked into another one already laying there. It was surprising how many apples were strewn around the tree trunk. Most looked like they'd been there for a while, browned and mushy.

Suddenly Mind and I both saw the ripest, juiciest apple. It made my mouth water. Mind got to it first and then started . . . not drooling . . . but blubbering!

What was the matter *now?* Surely not another caterpillar crisis?

Pooey LOVED apples! Mind remembered, sobbing between bites.

She *did* love apples. And that told me Mind *did* care. I held Mind's hand and stroked the back of it. Like me, Mind was scared about what was going to happen if we didn't find Pooey.

It was upsetting, but that hadn't stopped Mind from eating the apple. I *really* needed something in my belly too. So I crouched down and reached for an apple that looked fresh enough to eat, with no bug *protein* toppings, thank you! That's when I noticed the smallest bite marks you can imagine, in a couple of apples.

Something . . . some*one* . . . had been nibbling on them. They weren't like the holes caterpillars make when they tunnel through fruit, or the pecks of a bird's beak.

THEN I saw in the grass right next to the apples, what looked like . . .

POO!

Not just *any* poo, but . . .

RABBIT POO!

YES! At last! We'd found another CLUE! There were a few rabbit poos clumped together. They led to a TRAIL of poo! That could only mean *one* thing . . . Pooey had been here!

All we had to do now was FOLLOW the poo trail and it would lead us straight to Pooey! I jumped up as fast as I could and started following the poos, all the while being extra careful not to step on them.

Hold on. Mind stopped me in my tracks. Something wasn't quite right.

They were definitely Pooey's poos.

Pooey was *always* pooing in the garden, especially after munching on apples. There was no doubt about that.

But are these OLD poos or NEW poos?! Mind questioned.

There was no point following a trail of old poo from days ago.

That was just a waste of time.

'Good thinking, Mind!'

Maybe that nap and apple snack were just

what Mind needed to get back onto solving the mystery.

'Are you okay, Maya?' Anya asked.

I was so busy thinking about the poo, I hadn't noticed her following me.

Then I thought: Anya the animal lover was just the right person to help us out. She knew so much about animals; maybe she knew about animal poo too!

How could I ask Anya without telling her why I was suddenly so curious about poo?

I knew Mind didn't want me to tell anyone about Pooey. Mind had almost fallen out with me once over it. Now we were getting along again, I didn't want to mess that up. Maybe there was a way to ask for help without giving everything away.

Tanya skipped past. She was doing all sorts of fancy jumping tricks with her skipping rope.

I dreaded the thought of Tanya getting too close and messing up the poo trail. I was confident that Mind would help me keep the poo trail safe this time. Especially after what happened to us this morning with the poo trail in the kitchen.

But when I looked up, Mind was FLAPPING around in a panic!

GAAAAARRRRHHHHHHHH!

It was too much for Mind to take; the possibility of us losing this poo trail and any chance of ever finding Pooey. It was the ultimate nightmare scenario and felt like an utter CATASTROPHE waiting to happen!

Mind panted for breath and at the same time started to sprout tentacles, like an octopus out of water. One by one, they kept growing, until all eight of them were smattering grass and mud all over the place. At this rate, Mind was more likely to

smoosh the poo trail than Tanya!

The *only* way to stop all the skipping and flapping and octopus-ing – to save the poo from getting trampled on – was to get everyone's attention. So I stood up, raised my hands, and for once, shouted at the top of my voice so everyone could hear *exactly* what was on my mind:

'*STOPPP!!! SAVE THE POO!!!!!*'

It was such a *silly* and STRANGE thing to say, even Tanya had to STOP, to see and hear me.

Mind was still in a flap but got the message and managed to wibble-wobble away from the poo trail, over to the pond by the patio. At least Mind could cool off there.

I had surprised myself. In that moment, I didn't care what anyone thought. It was an emergency. And I did what I needed to. It had worked and the poo trail was safe! That was all that mattered.

But the moment after, I felt totally EMBARRASSED. I cleared my throat and tried to come up with something sensible.

'Ermmm, what I *mean* is . . . Pooey loves

SPLOSH!

to eat her own poo, so I don't want anyone to step on it. I want to save it for her.'

Everyone took their eyes off me and looked down at the rabbit poo.

Anya looked closer. 'I think rabbits only eat fresh poo'.

It was our chance to ask Anya, *Expert On All Things Animal*, about the poo!

'Oh really?' I asked. 'How do you know if the poo is old or new?'

'I'm not sure. Let me think . . .' Anya replied.

Tanya butted in – 'That's not the sort of thing you figure out by *thinking* . . . It's the sort of thing you figure out by *trying*.'

She cast her skipping rope aside.

'*New* poo is POO-IER than old poo!'

'What do you mean?' Anya grimaced.

'Follow me and I'll show you,' Tanya found a stick to call us over with.

Whew! Glad to be back! Mind had de-flapped and was brushing off a couple of suckers left from the tentacles that had dissolved away in the pond.

Mind picked two apples off the tree, one for each of us. Mind polished mine clean before offering it to me. I was *starving*. Mmm . . . it was sweet and gave me a rush of energy! That was more like *my* Mind, who looked out for me no matter what. I'd missed working together and was glad to be on the same team again. I gave Mind a hug. Then Mind started to listen in very carefully, scratching notes on a pad with an inky pen to keep track of what was going on.

'There's only ONE WAY to know if poo is old or new!' Tanya declared. 'There are two steps. First: **SSSMELL IT!** Second: **SSSQUISH IT!** The 'Two S Test' – that's what it's called.'

It was hard not to believe Tanya – after all, the 'Two S Test' sounded very proper. There was a name for it and everything. How could she be wrong?

That's too . . . Y U C KY . . . to be true. Mind thought (and hoped).

But Tanya was unstoppable: 'Now *you* TRY it!' She handed me the stick.

I bent down near one of the poos and tried to smell it.

'It doesn't *smell* of anything.' I was relieved but a bit confused – *why* wasn't it smelly?

Then, I tried prodding the same poo with the blunt end of the stick.

'I can't *squish* it . . .'

I tried poking another one. The poos were hard like pebbles.

'Aha!' Tanya swiped the stick away from me and made circles with it, like she was casting a spell with a magic wand. 'This poo has FAILED the 'Two S Test! That means it is . . . *OLD* POO!'

So much for our miraculous 'clue'!

But Mind had some questions. *How long does it take for new poo to become less poo-ey? What if this poo was smelly and squishy a few minutes ago, when it might have been brand new?!*

Mind pushed me to challenge Tanya.

'But the test doesn't tell you how old this poo is, compared to the newest, most pooey, poo.'

Tanya *didn't* like that. Not one bit.

'*You* won't know this yet Maya, because you're TOO *little* . . .' she said, as though being little was something terrible. 'The *correct* way of speaking is not to describe something as '*more* pooey' or '*most* pooey' . . . You *need* to learn to use SUPERLATIVES.'

Super-WHAT?? Mind almost gagged on a chunk of apple.

'POO-EY, POO-IER, POO-IEST!' Tanya belted out.

Excuse me? Mind didn't appreciate being spoken to that way. Mind was little too, just like me. The way Tanya said it made Mind and me feel like we were too little to matter.

This Tanya wasn't fun to play with. She was BOSSY. And Mind was NOT here to be bossed about. Even if Tanya was bigger and louder than us.

Tanya was always a *bit* bossy.

Well she's getting BOSS-ier by the day. And today, she's at her BOSS-iest. There!

Mind spouted stroppily. *Is that good enough for her?!*

I noticed spikes cropping up out of Mind's back. I gave Mind a gentle stroke, *before* we got anywhere near to another flap. It felt like Papa's face when his beard grew out on holiday . . . rough if you stroked it the wrong way, but nice and smooth the right way.

'If you can't say anything nice, don't say anything at all,' Anya reminded Tanya.

'Well, I don't think *you're* being very nice, so maybe *you* should SHUT UP!' Tanya puffed back at her.

PLOP! Something landed on Tanya's head.

'Now, THAT is definitely the POO-IEST bird poo of all!' Anya laughed.

Serves her right! Mind guffawed.

Tanya's face and neck turned redder than the apple I was holding.

I felt sorry for her. Everyone was trying to

help in their own way. *Even* Tanya.

I was just disappointed that we hadn't found another clue, after all. This time, Mind noticed how I was feeling. Mind patted my head: *On the bright side, at least there's no poo on you.*

CHAPTER 6

'The only thing I HATE more than animals, is their POO!' Tanya found a large maple leaf and tried to wipe the bird poo off her hair.

Anya tried to stand up for animals again. 'But the world *needs* animal poo. It helps us to . . .'

'NO MORE poo talk!' Tanya protested. 'Let's talk about what Maya's LOST instead!' She turned on me.

'Shhh . . . it's meant to be a secret that Maya's lost something,' Anya reminded her.

'If it's a SECRET and *no one* knows you've lost something, then *no one* knows you need to find something . . . so *no one* will EVER find it!' Tanya taunted.

'Maybe we can try to guess what you've lost?' Anya suggested.

Deep down, I was hoping they *would* guess.

Mind still did not agree. *If Tanya and Anya guess Pooey is lost, they'll have to tell Aunty Dolly, who will definitely tell Mama and Papa. Then we'll be in REAL trouble.*

I must have looked sad again.

'I know what Maya's LOST . . .' Tanya teased. 'She's lost her *smile!*'

I felt like crying right there and then.

Mind changed gear and fanned my face so my cheeks didn't turn red and not a single tear rolled down them. *No more guessing! No more games! No more playing with our feelings!*

'I'm booored,' Tanya groaned.

'I have an idea!' Anya smiled. 'Tanya, you're *always* losing things. Why don't you tell us how *you* find things when you've lost them?'

'Well, firstly, I *never* lose anything. But I *do* know what to do about it!' Tanya boasted.

'Where are your shoes?' Anya asked her.

Tanya glanced at her bare feet. She looked completely clueless.

'*If* I ever lost something, which I never do ... I would just go back in time to remember where I was and what I was doing when I lost it.'

'So, where are your shoes then?' Anya wouldn't let it go.

Tanya ignored Anya and went on.

'What better way to go back in time than

106

. . . in an *imaginary* TIME MACHINE!!'

No more games. Mind didn't want to see me getting upset again because of Tanya's gimmicks.

'It runs on MIND POWER! You have to use your imagination, otherwise it doesn't work.'

Tanya was really selling it to us. Mind liked the sound of *mind power.* And I thought anything that might help jog our memories and lighten the mood was a good thing.

'So . . . have a seat, close your eyes and make yourselves comfortable . . . I'll be your pilot today. Get ready for the ride of a lifetime!'

Part of me knew better than to keep listening to Tanya. And Mind still wasn't sure. But there was no harm in trying it . . . just for a test ride.

So, one at a time, we climbed into Tanya's time machine.

'All you have to do is think back to when you last saw my shoes . . .'

With my eyes shut, I thought hard.

'You took your shoes off in the treehouse!' My eyes popped open.

'YESSS!' Tanya cheered and clapped.

It felt *incredible* to be able to find something that was lost, so easily. Mind could tell I really wanted to give it a try to find Pooey. It was only make-believe anyway.

'Now think of whatever you've lost and tell me how far back in time it was so I can fly us there.' Tanya instructed.

I closed my eyes and tried to remember when I last saw Pooey.

'What are you thinking of?' Tanya was keen to get flying.

We can't tell her we're thinking of Pooey! Mind wasn't giving anything away and neither was I.

So I said, 'Nothing . . .'

Tanya grinned at mc, as if I'd said something *exhilarating*.

'I gucss we're going waaayyyyy back then . . . Hold on TIGHT!' She grabbed both my hands from behind me and dragged me backwards, shaking side to side.

'Remember, DO NOT open your eyes!'

It felt so uncomfortable to not be able to see anything while running at full speed and in reverse! Mind was clinging on to my back.

'Where are we going?' my voice waivered.
'Destination: **NOTHING!**'
I had no idea what Tanya was on about.
'You must have been thinking about a time *before* anything existed . . . millions

and billions and **TRILLIONS** of **YEARS AGOOO!!!**' she went on. 'Before The Big Bang! Back when there was **NOTHING!!!**'

'NO! That's *not* what I meant!' I told her, pulling my hands free before we went any further.

'Oh.' She stopped.

We came to a stand–still. I looked up. We had run all the way to the tallest conifer trees at the back of the garden. The sun and most of the sky had disappeared behind a huge dark cloud. Suddenly, it felt chilly.

'We've stopped *somewhere* on our journey through time . . .' Tanya told us. 'We are now . . . *somewhere* in the past . . . I'll need to check our exact location.'

Tanya started turning knobs and dialling buttons on the time machine. Mind's stomach was turning.

'Errr . . . I just saw something moving

behind those trees,' Anya sounded frightened.

'OH NO!' Tanya wailed, inching away. 'The time machine went WRONG. We're in BIG trouble now . . .'

'What do you mean?' I couldn't understand how an imaginary time machine could go wrong.

'This has NEVER happened to me before . . .'

Tanya admitting she didn't know something?! *That* was scary.

Mind felt sick.

'We haven't been transported to a time gone by . . . turns out we've got ourselves a visitor from another era.'

All the while, her eyes were locked on the tree in fear.

'Don't look now, but behind that tree . . . there's an ENORMOUS, pre-historic, *very* hungry-looking . . . D– d– d–' her voice trembled.

'D– d– d– ?!' I shivered.

Tanya's eyes bulged. She cupped her hands around her mouth and spelled out loud:

'D-I-N-O-S-A-U-R ! ! !'

'Dinosaur?' Anya was baffled. 'Tanya, stop messing around now.'

'For REAL!' Tanya gulped.

Impossible! Mind thought for a split second. But Tanya was so sure of herself.

'I *promise* you I'm not joking. But if you want to wait around to find out for yourselves . . .'

There was a **RUSTLE** in the bushes ahead of us. Then the leaves **SHOOK** just the way they would if a gigantic dinosaur was about to charge and . . .

EAT US ALIVE!!!

'RUN AWAYYYYYYYYYYYYY!!!!!!!!!!'
Anya shot past, grabbing my arm and pulling me along.

I wasn't about to take any chances. We all ran for our lives. I didn't look back even once. Whatever was chasing after us was terrifying enough for quiet, sensible Anya to shout louder than ever. That was enough to make me believe anything.

I ran and *ran* and *RAN* until we reached the house, where I knew we were safe. I'd never felt my heart beating so fast.

'Where's Tanya?!' I asked between breaths.

'Oh, don't worry – I'm fine,' we heard Tanya through the back door. She was sitting on the worktop in the laundry room. Her head was in the sink as she rinsed bird poo out of her hair. 'To tell you the truth, my imagination runs away with me sometimes.'

Her imagination had us all running – that was for sure!

'So there *was* no dinosaur and we should *never* believe you again.' Anya concluded. 'Liar, *liar*, Pilot Tanya should be *fired!*'

How could she lie like that and trick us into believing something completely untrue?

Then I remembered I had lied to Papa too. What if he didn't believe me ever again after today?

Mind was starting to think telling a lie (even just one) wasn't such a good idea after all. But keeping secrets hadn't helped either.

CHAPTER 7

We were running out of time. We had no idea where Pooey was, and we needed help!

The washing machine whirred and spun around. The clock resting on it beeped. I couldn't believe it was 12 noon already. Every *tick* and *tock* of the clock seemed more URGENT. As a matter of fact, with every passing minute, Pooey could be getting *more* LOST . . . and harder to find!

It was clear to me that we HAD to tell Tanya and Anya that Pooey was lost, so they could help us find her . . . before it was too late.

I tried to explain, but Mind wouldn't

listen to me. No matter what I had to say, Mind didn't want to hear it.

According to Mind, none of this was a matter of *fact* . . . it was a matter of *opinion*. Just because *my* worst fear was losing Pooey forever, didn't mean that was actually going to happen. And just because I would *feel* better by telling someone Pooey was lost, didn't mean that telling someone would actually make things better.

Stop going on about it. We're better off looking for Pooey by ourselves, in our own way.

Mind made me feel like *my* opinion didn't count . . . And if Mind was going to be like that, then in my OPINION, Mind was being a BIG BABY. Mind needed to *grow up*.

'Bottom line: You're more worried about getting told off than finding Pooey. It's ALL your FAULT we're in this mess.'

That's it! I'm done!

Mind had had ENOUGH of being blamed for everything and I had had enough of Mind, full stop. So off we went, on our own separate ways. I was so upset that I didn't even care where Mind was going.

'Hey, where are you going, Maya?' Anya called out. But I didn't stop. I didn't want to talk to anyone.

I kept stomping until I reached the end of the garden again, by the tall trees. There was nowhere left to go. I looked back. The house was so far away and seemed so small, like a drawing. Everything looked right . . . right where it should be. The bricks all in their rows, neat square window frames, and a chimney on top. Only I knew everything was not where it should be. Pooey was missing. So even if everything else looked perfectly fine, nothing *felt* right.

If I couldn't tell anyone about it, at least I could stomp about it. So that's what I did. Stomp. Stomp! STOMP! **SQUELCH.**

I looked down at my foot. There was something icky between my toes . . . something *smelly* and *squishy*. That's when

I saw, there in the grass . . .

. . . LOTS of little rabbit poos.

But this time, the poos looked different. I tried to remember what Tanya had taught us about the 'Two S Test' – Smell and Squish. I checked no one was looking and picked up a twig.

I leaned in, so my nose was as close to the poo as I could get without touching the poo.

It was . . . *SMELLY!!!*

Next, I held the twig tightly and pushed it into the poo.

It was . . . *SQUISHY!!!*

The poo had PASSED Tanya's 'Two S Test' . . . !

That meant this rabbit poo was NEW! This was a NEW POO TRAIL, freshly made by Pooey. It led straight into the bushes under the tall trees. Suddenly, I remembered the RUSTLE we heard before. Of course it wasn't a dinosaur! It was POOEY!!!

I bolted over and got down on my hands and knees to follow the poo trail, as far as I could, under the branches and leaves. It went right up to the garden fence . . . but that was where the poo trail ended. The ground had been dug up. Pooey had burrowed *under* the fence and *out* of the garden.

How could we have let this happen?! Pooey had probably been right in front of our eyes and instead of looking for her in the bushes, we ran the other away!

If only Mind hadn't stopped me doing what felt right all along . . . if only I'd told someone the TRUTH about Pooey being lost . . . we could have looked for her together and found her while she was in the garden. Who knew where she was by now?? What if my worst FEAR had come true?!

I walked back to the house, feeling bluer than ever. How could I not remember when or where I last saw Pooey? Why did I fall out with Mind? How could Mind storm off like that and leave me to solve the mystery all by myself?

In the living room, Mama, Aunty Dolly, Tanya and Anya were all sitting on their yoga mats with their legs crossed. I stood by the wall and watched.

Mama said softly, 'Now, take a deeeeep breath in . . . and *clear* your mind . . .'

I *would* if only Mind hadn't decided to *clear off!*

Mind strolled in and made a point of sitting at the opposite end of the room from me, looking the other way and acting

like I didn't exist.

Mama stood on one leg, like a flamingo. She looked so elegant. Then Aunty Dolly and the twins joined her. They made it look easy to balance on one foot like that. I tried to copy them but it was tough without Mind by my side. I swayed forwards and backwards, my arms and legs making jerky movements . . . then I lost my balance altogether and nearly fell over. I looked more like a flamingo on ice!

BAHAHAHAAAAA!!!

Mind laughed out loud. Well, at least that was better than ignoring me.

It *was* funny but Mind didn't want to see me fall and get hurt. Mind got up and showed me how to move in true *diva* style. Mind did the smoothest one foot glide across the room. Then Mind skated in figures of 8 around the room, followed by a set of twizzles towards me . . . all with flawless footwork, as if it came naturally. My jaw crashed to the floor so hard that if we were on a real ice rink, it would have smashed straight through.

'Since when did you become an ice-skating pro?!'

Mind blushed.

Don't over-think it. Just loosen up and give it a go! Mind whizzed by again, arms twisting through the air like a ballerina and skates slicing through the ice like they were an extension of Mind's self.

Mind made space for me, laying out my very own yoga mat.

So I tried to do the Flamingo again, this time with Mind's help to keep me steady.

Everything clicked into place. I could only do it with Mind and me working together. A bit of team work and we got it – the perfect BALANCE!

We were both sorry. We had both made mistakes. It made me smile to think we were at our BEST together.

'If we can figure out yoga together, we can do *anything* . . .'

I'll bet we can even find Pooey!

I made room for Mind to join me sitting next to Mama. I crossed my legs and closed my eyes, just like her. Then we breathed in and out slooowly, counting *1 . . . 2 . . . 3 . . . 4 . . .*

It was the first time since we'd woken up today that Mind was completely still and silent. Everything felt clearer.

A happy memory came to Mind. It was a memory of the first time I ever saw Pooey . . . a baby rabbit at the farm. She fit in my hands, with large, chocolatey brown eyes and floppy ears. Her fur was strawberry blonde with gingerbread biscuit coloured

patches on her back. I fed her some hay and she left a couple of warm rabbit poos in my palms. So that was the name I gave her: Pooey.

'That was the *first* time we saw Pooey . . . But when was the *last* time we saw her?'

In the quiet, I heard something . . . a *rustling* sound. I wasn't sure what it was, but it sounded like something I'd heard before. I stayed put, while Mind followed the sound up the stairs and into my room.

There, Mind found a memory buried away under all the chaos. It was a memory from last night when I was getting ready for bed . . .

Pooey was in her hutch *rustling* around in her hay. I had put her back in her hutch, like I always do at the end of the day. I was about to close the hutch door and then I got distracted by a clattering outside. From my window we saw Papa setting up the trampoline in the back garden . . . So we *flew* downstairs and into the garden for some trampoline time before bed time!

OH NO . . .

I FORGOT TO CLOSE POOEY'S HUTCH DOOR!!!!

So *that* was how Pooey had gone missing. Of course she hadn't opened the hutch door by herself! And *that* was why Mind was up so early this morning . . .

I knew something was wrong. I knew we hadn't done something we should've the night before . . . I just couldn't work out what it was!

I imagined myself stroking the fluffy bit between baby Pooey's ears once more. That always relaxed her. Her oval eyes blinked sleepily and her nose stopped twitching.

I rested my cheek against her forehead. She smelt of . . .

GINGER?!

The sweet scent of spiced tea woke me up from day-dreaming about Pooey. It was a mix of ginger, cinnamon, cardamom and cloves. Whenever the grown-ups had their masala chai they made sure all us kids got our mango lassi! It was the YUMMIEST milkshake, especially when we visited India in the summer. There was something about Indian mangoes blended into thick, creamy buffalo milk, served with ice cubes bobbing up and down in a shiny steel glass, that no other milkshake came close to. I couldn't DREAM of a better treat.

Rain spattered against the front door and the windows.

Looks like everyone else finished with yoga a looong time ago!

I wondered how long I'd been sitting there by myself, lost in my own thoughts.

'Maya! Come join us, we're having *chai . . .*' Mama called me to the dining table. As expected, that was followed by: 'Aunty Dolly's made some MANGO *LASSI* for you!'

She *knew* that was the fastest way to get me to go anywhere.

At the table, Papa was passing a plate of veggie *pakoras* around.

'Phooey!' Tanya pinched her nose at the food.

Aunty Dolly reminded her not to be rude.

All Mind heard was: *Phooey*. But all *I* could think of was: **POOEY.**

Once the thoughts started going around in my head, I couldn't stop them . . . Pooey was lost and it was MY FAULT. Now, Pooey was out on the streets, left to defend herself against all sorts of DANGER. And I wasn't even brave enough to tell anyone that Pooey was missing. Here I was, chilling at home and looking forward to a treat!

You deserve a treat. WE deserve a treat. Mind nudged me to sit. *Now that we've remembered exactly what happened, we can finally tell everyone!*

But now, *I* was the one who needed convincing.

Mama poured me a glass of lassi and Anya passed my favourite straw – the one shaped like a bunny.

Maybe I could tell everyone the straw reminded me I needed to go check on Pooey . . . then I could sneak off to my room and pretend I *just* discovered Pooey was missing. That way, it couldn't be *our* fault (we've been out playing all morning). And I wouldn't have to admit I'd lied.

No. More. Lies. Mind was set. *Lies – no! Lassi – yes!*

'What's up?' Aunty Dolly leaned over. 'You don't seem your usual self today.'

Aunty Dolly was always spot on about how you were feeling. She could take one look into your eyes and gauge the *exact* feeling inside you – out of ALL the never-ending list of possible feelings a person can feel. It was almost as if she had an inbuilt Feelings Finding Radar. Hopefully she couldn't see straight through me and tell how I was feeling about lying! I tried to avoid making eye contact just in case her radar readings went off the wall, finding me: GUILTY!

Maybe it's just because you haven't touched your lassi yet . . . Mind was right. That would give away that something was up with me, to just about anyone.

I forced a smile, then put my straw in my mouth so no one would ask me any more questions.

Tanya licked the foamy mango *lassi* off her top lip. Then she announced out of nowhere:

'Maya's lost something but she won't say what it is!'

'Oh?' Mama looked surprised.

'We were only playing a game,' Anya covered for me.

That was a *close call!*

I blew bubbles into the last bit of *lassi* at the bottom of my glass so I didn't have to look up at anyone. I was *still* not ready to tell everyone that I'd lost Pooey. Mind couldn't understand why. *What have we got to lose?*

Thinking back to when I'd lost things

135

before, it was HUMILIATING. The *worst* feeling.

When you lose something at school, they parade it on stage in assembly, with all the other Lost & Found stuff. Like a fashion show for losers. You have to go to the Head Teacher's office to claim your things, as if losing your own belongings was something you'd do on purpose to be naughty. But the Headteacher isn't the problem. It's Mr Strict (that's what everyone calls him – even the parents). He mans the office doors. You have to get past *him* first. He always looks ready to tell somebody off. I'll never forget the first time his scratchy voice wiped the smile off my face, when I went to collect my jacket: 'So, you're not the *golden girl* we all thought you were!'

'Maya was up very early this morning . . .' Mama's voice brought me back to the table.

'You wanted to give me a nice surprise,' Papa smiled. 'Didn't you?'

Errrrrm . . . did I??

If I *did*, I had forgot all about it by now. There was only *one* surprise this morning that I could remember right now . . . and it was *not* a nice one. Waking up to find Pooey had disappeared!

'Maya, why don't you tell Aunty Dolly what you wanted to surprise me with this morning?' Papa put me on the spot.

Mind was slurping on mango *lassi* with a look that said: *Time. To. Tell. The. Truth.*

How could I tell the truth *now* . . . in front of everyone? If I *could*, I would. It would make life so much easier! But I didn't know how to tell them the truth and I couldn't remember all the lies I'd told . . . I was lost for words.

Thankfully, Aunty Dolly saved the day.

'Hmmmmm . . .' she hummed like a bird. 'I think it's *time* . . . for a Maya *rhyme* . . .'

Maya is a LIAR was the only rhyme I thought fit.

But as always, Aunty Dolly was about to turn something not-so-fun, into something so-so-FUN for everyone –

'Maya The Flyer, was up all night,
She snuck out early, before daylight . . .
She took her Papa's magic kite,
Up on the hill for a magical flight!

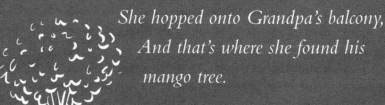

She clung to it tight and flew away!
Landing five thousand miles away . . .
She hopped onto Grandpa's balcony,
And that's where she found his
mango tree.

Wasting no time, Maya did climb,
Until she reached the very top,
To pluck the best mangoes of the lot!
Keen to get back before Papa knew,
Maya got back on the kite and flew . . .

Maya The Flyer was up in the air,
She reached back home
Just in time to prepare . . .
The most special surprise –
Yes, it shows . . .
She chose the sweetest,
yummiest mangoes!

So Maya might have lost something,
But look what she found . . .
She only went and got us
The best mangoes around!'

She raised her glass of mango lassi.

'Awwwww that was lovely!' Mama gushed, 'Cheers, everyone! To Maya!'

We all reached around to *cheers* each other. Everyone joined in at once, arms stretching over from all directions. CLINK! Papa stood up and his plate flipped off the edge of the table. *Pakoras* FLEW everywhere. Trying to catch them, Mama knocked over the jug and a fountain of lassi showered onto Tanya's lap, making her jump. That toppled the bowl of banana chips over like a chest of gold coins, crashing into spoons that catapulted dipping sauces everywhere. Green chutney was slung Anya's way, like a blotchy face mask gone wrong.

The whole room went silent. No one dared make another move.

A splodge of coconut chutney dripped from the ceiling. Everyone looked up.

Aunty Dolly took her glasses off and licked the chutney off them, as if it was all perfectly normal.

'Mm-mmm . . . Tastes even better served off the ceiling!'

That made Mind giggle . . . which made *me* giggle . . . and soon *everyone* was giggling around the table.

'If Pooey was here, I'm pretty sure she would be giggling too!' I smiled.

It felt good to say Pooey's name out loud. Talking about her made it feel like she was still here. And maybe she would be again.

Seeing everyone happy made me happier. Imagining Pooey happy, made me the happiest of all. I didn't feel so blue anymore.

Aunty Dolly had a way of sprinkling happiness over everyone. She shared the feeling she was feeling, so other people could feel it too. She always said that it was only after she'd been down that she had learned how to get back *up* again. No matter how bad things seemed, there was always a reason to smile. She never gave up. We just needed to be more like her!

CHAPTER 8

Mind was full of hope. Surely now that we had figured out *how* Pooey got lost, we would be able to figure out how to find her. Why waste time feeling *bad* about losing Pooey, when we could use that time to do something good . . . like FIND her! I was beginning to believe we could do it. Suddenly, the impossible seemed possible. Mind whooped excitedly!

We left the table while everyone was busy passing around tissues and clearing away. Running up to my room, we started forming a *new* plan to find Pooey.

The conversation downstairs had got

me thinking.

'I've lost *and* found things before!'

That's for sure!

The more I thought about it, the more I figured Pooey going missing wasn't all that different to when other things went missing. Sometimes books fell behind the bookshelf, where I couldn't see them, or toys rolled under the bed and out of sight.

'What if Pooey's already made her way back home after digging her way out of the garden? What if she's hiding under my bed *right now?!*'

I lifted my blanket, and we looked under the bed – no Pooey. Behind the bookshelf? Nope. Pooey wasn't there either.

'Whenever I've lost things before, I've always found them right where I left them.'

But those were things, Mind reminded me. *Things get lost and found. Pooey isn't a THING.*

Mind was right. Pooey was part of our family. I saw her empty hutch again.

'We've looked everywhere – inside and outside. Even back in time, according to Tanya!

And still, there's been no sign of Pooey anywhere.'

RATATATATA . . . BRRRRSSSSHHHH!!!

Streaming down the window, it looked like the sky was crying.

Poor Pooey . . . she's probably dripping wet and cold, somewhere far away from home.

'What if something's happened to her?'

WHAT IF the neighbour's *evil* cat had caught her?!

I felt my cheeks go hot and red. My eyes filled up and before I knew it . . . a big tear rolled down my face. First, there was just one. I wiped it away. Then I blinked. Two more. Then all at once there were so many tears, I couldn't stop crying.

THIS IS THE WORST DAY EVER.
Mind bawled.

Papa walked in.

'What's the matter, Maya?'

I hadn't even heard him coming upstairs.
Not that it mattered anymore.

'I can't find Pooey . . .' I cried.

Papa looked over at the empty hutch.

'I'm sorry I lied to you this morning,'
I sniffled.

Telling lies felt *so* easy at the time. But
it didn't help. It only made things worse,
and spending the whole day trying to keep
secrets from everyone was hard work.

It wasn't worth it!

I told him everything.

'When I got up this morning I saw Pooey
was gone, so I tried to find her by myself.
When Tanya and Anya came over, I told

them I lost something but I was too scared to tell them it was Pooey . . . I thought they might tell on me . . .' I blubbed.

Mind sat down next to me and put a hand on my shoulder, in solidarity. We were in this together.

'Then . . . I found more rabbit poo in the garden and I followed it to try and find Pooey . . . but it was too late! Pooey must have dug her way out under the fence and it's all my fault . . . because *I* left her hutch door open!'

'It's okay, Maya,' Papa gave me a hug. 'The good thing is you've told me the truth now. We'll find Pooey together. She can't have gone far. Let's go tell Mama so she can help too.'

Pinching my cheeks with his chunky fingers, he chirped in German, '*Vielen Dank, für die . . . Bluuuuu-men!*'

It meant, 'Thank you for the flowers'. At the end of the day, if nothing else, we could always be happy about the flowers. Ever since I was a baby, he'd said it to help me look on the bright side. And it still worked.

Mind, teary-eyed, leaned in for a group hug. Finally, we were FREE of the load we'd been carrying all day. *Lies felt so* **HEAVY.**

We went downstairs.

'Aunty Dolly and the girls just left,' Mama told us. 'They wanted to say bye-bye but they were getting late for bowling.'

Whenever they left it felt like a party was over.

We sat down with Mama and told her that Pooey was missing. I told her the whole story. At first, Mama didn't say anything. I wondered if she was cross.

'Maya, I'm so happy that you told us. That's all that matters,' she said.

'But I did something wrong . . . telling lies is wrong.' I still felt bad about it, even though Mama and Papa were being so nice.

'Well, you also did something right, by telling the truth now and asking for help,' Papa pointed out.

Mind couldn't agree more and applauded us. *With the Dream Team on the case, we still have a chance of finding Pooey before the end of the day!*

'*Sunoh* . . .' Mama wanted me to listen. '*Everyone* makes mistakes. I'll let you in on a *secret* of my own . . .' I loved when Mama said that. It always made me look at her differently.

'The truth is, when *I* was a little girl like you, one time in India . . . I left Grandpa's balcony door open and his pet parrot escaped. He flew away right in front of me! I only 'fessed up in the end because when we found him, he kept threatening to tell on me: *Polly gonna tell on ya!*'

Really?! Mind couldn't imagine Mama ever doing anything like that. We wouldn't have believed it if she hadn't told us herself.

'Yup. That was the very first thing he said to me when the neighbours brought him back days later. No *hello* or *nice to be home!*

Cheeky chappy that *tota*.  That's parrot in Hindi.' Mama never missed a chance to teach me a new word.

'I've got one too . . .' Papa pitched in. 'Not a parrot; but a confession. I made a BIG mistake with those *pakoras* today. I put WAY more salt in that batter than I meant to. Lucky most of them ended up on the floor, I guess.'

I knew Papa was *trying* to help me feel better but I also knew what I did was much worse than making pakoras too salty.

'I'm surprised to hear that,' Mama frowned at Papa. She sounded disappointed.

Uh-oh thought Mind . . . *Let's hope the Dream Team isn't about to fall apart!*

'I'm *surprised* because I thought the pakoras were delicious!'

Phew! Mind was relieved.

'I'm also surprised Pooey ran away,' Mama added, more serious now.

My *worst* thought came to Mind.

Mind wasn't sure we should say it out loud though. But, so far, telling Mama and Papa things felt better than not telling them. Every time I told them something I thought was *really* bad, they helped me see it was not-so-bad after all. So I decided to share my worst thought:

'Do you think Pooey is gone forever?'

'It sounds to me like Pooey might be in someone else's garden. If she dug under the fence, she's probably blissfully nibbling away on Mrs Gill's best blooms!' Mama said brightly.

'Or those prize carrots that win Mr Rao across the way first place in the Greenest Garden Competition *every* single year . . .' Papa muttered to himself.

Let's find Pooey together. We can do it!
Mind was confident now. *After all, you're magical Maya the Flyer!*

That's when I came up with a TOP idea – FLYERS! We could hand them out to all the neighbours. If *everyone* kept an eye out, that meant a LOT more eyes looking out for Pooey than just Mind and me trying to find her on our own . . . It was WAY better than any of the ideas we'd come up with when we were looking for Pooey on our own. I only wished I had told Mama and Papa about Pooey sooner.

Mama and Papa were all for it . . . but then, out of nowhere, Papa said – 'There is just ONE problem with the plan . . .'

Oh no. What was it now?!

'How are you going to deliver flyers with just one sock on?' He tickled the toes on my bare foot and pulled a funny face.

'Papaaa! This is no time for jokes. We've got work to do.'

We got some paper and my arts and crafts bag. With Mind's help, I drew a picture of Pooey from memory. Making things always felt so good. Holding Pooey's picture close to me, it almost felt like we were together again. Papa helped me with the words and then he printed out a dozen copies of the flyer we'd made.

Downstairs, Mama was heating up frozen samosas in the microwave for us to take

along. I was so hungry and Mind was so keen to get going, that we pocketed a packet of crisps and headed out.

'You can wait outside but raincoat and wellies on first and no further than the driveway please!'

Even though we hadn't found Pooey yet, I already felt better. I had a clear conscience, a plan to find Pooey and I was about to fill my belly!

As soon as I stepped out, I could see, hear and *feel* all the dangerous things that Pooey must have seen, heard and felt. Cars whizzed past on the road, spraying muddy puddles onto the pavement. A cold raindrop trickled down my neck.

SHOOP-SHWOOP! SHOOP-SHWOOP!
Mind swept the rain water off the drive, just like the road sweepers in monsoon season in India.

The clouds thundered, grey and stormy now.

'Let's wait in the back garden for Mama and Papa,' I shivered.

They always take forever to get out of the house! Mind mumbled impatiently.

'They're probably packing a bag full of things we need.'

And things we don't need! Mind added with an eye roll.

That got me worried enough to double check we'd taken the flyers. I unzipped my bag just a tiny bit to peek inside. They wouldn't be much use if we left them at home. So many things seemed to get left behind on the kitchen table whenever we went out. It made me wonder sometimes whether there was a forcefield around that table that made things invisible as soon as you put them there. Then when you came back later you could see them again and they'd been right there all along (but only after you'd worked yourself up and wasted all your time and effort looking everywhere else first).

Maybe that's where we left Pooey – on the kitchen table! Mind joked.

I didn't think it was very funny at all and nervously took one of the flyers out, trying not to get the rest soaked. I couldn't remember now if we had put Pooey's name on it.

Mind was bored of waiting and wandered off down the garden. I followed a few paces behind and took out my umbrella to try to keep dry while admiring the flyer we'd made. With one hand, I turned to the bit that had my drawing of Pooey across the middle. Raindrops splish–splashed onto Pooey's face, making the paper wet and soggy. I folded the damp flyer and tucked it away in my pocket. With both hands free, I held the umbrella steady and looked up to see where Mind was taking us.

Mind had transformed, standing tall and leafy with the odd branch sticking out here and there, looking exactly how you might imagine a tree to look . . . if it had turned into a dinosaur.

I'm a **DINOSAUR . . . RAAAAAAARRR!** Hunched over, with arms bent tight and clawing in the air with both hands, Mind growled at nothing and stomped around, going nowhere. Mind was playing tricks on me, but luckily this time I knew it wasn't a real dinosaur.

Can't believe you actually thought there was a real dinosaur in a tree!

'Well, *actually* I didn't think it was in a tree. I thought there was a dinosaur *behind* a tree.'

Do you know how strange that sounds?!

'Not as strange as *you* sounded just then trying to be a dinosaur . . .'

RUSTLE!

Speaking of strange sounds . . . What was THAT?!

RUSTLE! We heard again. This time, I recognised the sound. It wasn't strange at all.

It was a sound I knew well. But what was it??

It wasn't the rustle of crisps we had taken from the kitchen as we left the house, for us to snack on. Mind turned the empty packet over with a guilty face – nothing left to rustle in *there!*

And it wasn't the rustle of leaves blowing in the wind. Mind licked a finger and pointed it up to the sky. The air was perfectly still – not even the slightest bit of breeze to rustle a single leaf.

But the leaves were in fact moving . . . This time, there really was something behind those bushes under the trees.

RUSTLE! It went one more time, sparking my memory –

Pooey!

Of course! It was the same rustling sound she'd made when we were in the garden earlier, that we mistook for a dinosaur. The same rustling sound of Pooey in her hutch that woke me up every morning.

Mind rejoiced, sparkling like a firework in celebration. It was the best thing we'd heard all day!

'Shhh . . .' I reminded Mind, as the

sparkler burnt out.

'We have to be quiet if we're going to catch Pooey. The last thing we want to do is scare her away again.'

Mind nodded along quietly but inside we were still bursting with excitement at the thought of it. We'd solved the mystery!

We couldn't see Pooey yet but Mind was sure she was just a few steps out of our reach, not too far at all.

We did it! All by ourselves!

Mind patted me on the back a tad too hard and I fell forwards.

'Wooooaaahh!'

I skidded on a wet leaf like a slippery banana skin under my foot and landed right in the bushes.

Pooey rustled away, deeper into the darkness between the thickest, thorniest branches . . . even *further* out of reach.

Mind was in a state of shock, hands up in the air like someone caught doing something they know they shouldn't.

Whoops. Sorryyy!

We had to stay calm. We'd done better when we were calm than when we were in a flap. We'd come so far in our search for Pooey when we worked together (and we got nowhere when we fell out). So I took a deep breath and whispered:

'It's OK . . . Let's follow the rustling.'

We got as low down to the ground as possible, onto our elbows, and crawled in as far as we could, until I couldn't get any further. Mind wedged into the tiniest gap to get a closer look. There . . . was a little ball of a tail. Forcing a way in, Mind could just about make out a small round furry bum. As fluffy and gingerish as ever . . .

POOEY!

Hooorrraaaaaaayyyyyyyy!!!! Mind was ready to party, like a big rocket firework lighting up the sky.

Mind started to imagine hundreds, if not thousands, of different ways to get to Pooey. I felt my heart racing like a horse inside my chest. But even if Mind could reach Pooey, how would we pull her out?!

This'll get Pooey out from under there!
5 . . . 4 . . . 3 . . . 2 . . . 1 . . .
Mind began counting down to lift off. I could see it now . . . Mind exploding in the air with a BANG loud enough to make anyone dash away in surprise.

But, WAIT! What if Pooey didn't run out of the bushes but got such a fright that she burrowed underground and escaped again?!

We couldn't risk making a wrong move. We had to think about this *very* carefully. Mind wasn't thrilled about me being such a drag.

'As soon as we get hold of Pooey . . . it's party time,' I reassured Mind.

Thankfully, that was all Mind needed to hear to feel like it was worth the wait.

Pooey was trapped in a locked cage covered in thorns, with no key or door to let her out.

At least she's safe in there . . . you know, from the rain and all the dangerous things outside . . . Mind tried to stay positive.

Then, right on cue, we heard a muffled *miaow*.

It's that pesky cat again from the neighbour's garden! Mind peered out above the canopy. *She's heading over! She must have smelled Pooey from a distance and followed her nose.*

It was coming up to teatime and Pooey probably smelled yummy to a peckish cat. We needed to make sure Pooey wasn't on today's menu!

'We have to chase off that cat before she finds Pooey.'

I shuffled backwards through the dirt and leaves, popping out of the bushes like a crab out of the sand on the seashore. Blinking in the daylight, I squinted at the cat. She greeted us with a menacing 'Miaaooow!'

'Go on! Go away!' We shooed her away as quickly and quietly as we could.

She slunk back out of our garden through a crack in the fence. Mind marvelled at the cat getting her whole body through the narrowest slit in the wooden panel.

'Hey! That's it!'

What's what?

'That's how we're going to get Pooey out! Pooey is all fur, just like that cat. She can fit through the teeniest, weeniest spaces. All we need is something to tempt her out of there and I've got just the thing for it.'

I eyed the apple trees and wondered how to get an apple while staying put so we could still keep a close eye on Pooey.

Mind curled up around the biggest rock I could find to throw. I took aim and hurled it at an apple tree, like a bowling ball at the alley where Anya and Tanya had their birthday party every year. Mind and the rock solid ball spun forwards together. **STRIKE!** They smashed into a pile of apples at the foot of the tree, knocking them up into the air. One rebounded off another.

THWACK! A hard red apple hurtled in my direction, just like a cricket ball. I cupped my hands together the way that top fielders do and caught it! Mind had switched from bowling to cricket faster than I could say...

HOWZZZAT!!! That's what the bowler shouts, isn't it?!

A flood of memories came back to Mind and me. It felt as strong and as real as the rain. It was the summer we'd visited India to watch a Cricket World Cup match in the biggest stadium in the world. It was packed full of people dancing and cheering, the air filled with sounds of whistles and horns, and the colours of the teams waving on banners and on painted faces. Papa had said it was 'electrifying' being there. Even though I didn't know what the word meant, I knew exactly how it felt.

We'd never played cricket before. Bowling, tennis, football, basketball – yes. But CRICKET?! It was a whole new ball game for us. It was a bit like rounders or baseball, where one team bowls a ball and the other team bats to hit the ball. For the bowling side, the way to win is to hit the wicket. It sounds very simple but can be *extremely* hard to do.

Hit the WICKET to win at CRICKET! Hit

the wicket to win at cricket! Hit the wicket . . .
Mind chanted.

Suddenly, it was like we were playing the match of our lives, here and now. One final ball left to bowl in the Pooey World Cup; we were in it to win it, tired and drenched (not in sweat, but rain, in our case); in a race against time, with everything left to play for . . .

In the bushes, right where we needed to get the apple close enough to lure Pooey

out, there were three branches sticking out of the ground . . .

The wicket!

I had ONE shot. If the apple went too far, it would scare Pooey off. If it didn't go far enough, Pooey wouldn't be able to see or smell the treat to follow it out of the bushes. It was all on me now. The LAST ball of the innings.

It felt like we were *very* close to winning. And with a prize as special as Pooey . . .

GAME ON!

I gave the apple a quick toss in the air for luck (the way world class bowlers do). Then I took a bite out of it. Mind raised an eyebrow at me. We'd never seen anyone *bite* the ball before. I figured it might help Pooey pick up the apple-y scent.

Then I went into full-on cricketer mode. An impressive run-up . . . I launched myself into the air and swung my arms forward with a skip–hop–jump move (the type of move you only ever see the best-of-the-best bowlers doing).

With a masterful flick of my wrist, I let the apple go! We watched it roll under the bush and it stopped *exactly* where we wanted it to. Mind and I cheered under our breath. Then, we waited.

Nothing. No rustling. No sign of Pooey.

Just as we were about to give up . . .

One very gingerish twitching nose appeared, with whiskers quivering around it . . . two floppy ears followed and then, hopping out with both her front paws . . .

'Pooey!'

She sniffed at the apple. I reached down and gently ran two fingers, from the tip of her nose to her ears and all the way along her soft, round back — just to be sure I wasn't dreaming.

She looked fine. It was as if nothing had happened.

I bundled Pooey up in my jacket and carried her back to the house. Holding her up like a trophy, with the glow of the win on our faces, and imagining how happy Mama and Papa would be when we got back, like homecoming champions . . . we did a victory lap around the garden and stormed through the gate into the driveway, ready to celebrate.

But, at the front door, Mama was busy rooting around in her big bag she always took with her whenever she left the house (who knows why . . . she can never find anything in it when she needs to). And Papa was fumbling with the keys in his rush to lock up.

'Mama! Papa!' I called out. 'It's Pooey!'

They both stopped what they were doing. Papa dropped the keys. Mama even dropped her bag.

I could tell they couldn't believe it.

It was like we'd done a magic trick. Except, instead of making a rabbit appear out of a hat, Pooey stuck her head out of my jacket!

TA-DAAAH!

She twitched her nose at them.

'POOEY!' they rushed over.

WOW! Mind still couldn't believe it.

We imagined everything from pirate ships and treasure hunts, to riding horses, flying time machines and dinosaurs . . . But we never could have imagined the worst day ever would turn out to be **THE BEST DAY EVER!**

Mind gave me a high five!

Go Mind and me! We had solved the mystery together (with a bit of help along the way).

It really didn't matter who'd lost Pooey or who'd found Pooey. The only thing that mattered was that she was back home, safe and sound, where she belonged.

Telling lies felt like the easiest thing to do but it was the WORST thing I'd done . . . while telling the *truth* felt like the hardest thing to do but it was the BEST thing I'd done.

'Well, I think we've all learned something important today.' Papa picked the keys up off the ground.

'I've learnt that I need a smaller bag!' Mama sighed, dipping her hand into her bag again.

'Anyone learnt anything else?' Papa looked at us, as he opened the door and kicked the muck off his shoes on the rough mat.

We'd just won a World Cup! We'd learnt *so* many new things. Mind frantically jotted down everything we'd learnt in pretty little cards, like thank you notes. Mind hurriedly passed them to me, attached to bunches of flowers. Each was different and special in its own way. I picked one and proudly read it out loud:

'I've learnt . . . I want to start a cricket club at school?!'

Mind gulped awkwardly and slid out of sight.

Papa wasn't sure what to say to that. Neither was *I* to be honest!

So I handed him Pooey instead. He

stroked the soft furry bit between her ears and then smiled at me. I hopped into Papa's arms just as happily as Pooey had hopped back into mine.

'I'm sure we can find Grandpa's old cricket bat, can't we?' Papa said, looking over at Mama.

'Not if it's in this bag!' Mama huffed and finally looked up. She put the bag on the kitchen table as if she wished it *would* disappear.

Mama juggled a couple of hot samosas wrapped in foil and Mind roller-skated back onto the scene, grateful for food.

Ahhh . . . Vielen Dank für die SAMOSAS!!!

'Right. Time for bed, everyone!'

Pooey led the way upstairs and we followed her – this time hoping she *wasn't* leaving a trail of poo behind.

Pooey didn't seem bothered, but today

was a day I'll *never* forget.

Speaking of never forgetting things . . .

Now that it's bedtime for Mind and me, we had better just check one last time . . . that we've closed the hutch door!

DEDICATION

This book is for Shreya and Aarav.
Always remember the power and
magic of your mind.

To Gaurav for dreaming with me,
and to Sandeep and Deepak for
the memories.

Special thanks to my Mama and Papa
for believing in my mind and me –
Vielen Dank für die Blumen!

ACKNOWLEDGEMENTS

Thank you to Lucy, Eishar and Sophie.

SUNITA CHAWDHARY
AUTHOR & ILLUSTRATOR

Sunita Chawdhary is a British–Indian author-illustrator, doctor, and mum of two, based in Yorkshire. She studied art and design at Central Saint Martins. Sunita draws on her experience of growing up in Asia, America and Europe to create vibrant, multicultural worlds filled with diverse characters and stories. She believes that children of all cultures and backgrounds should see themselves represented in print. Sunita was commended for the Faber Andlyn BAME (FAB) prize in 2019. She has illustrated the Together We Can Change the World series of picture books, focusing on love and community in all corners of the world. The first title, *Pedro the Puerto Rican Parrot*, was published by Little Steps in April 2021.

KNIGHTS OF

KNIGHTS OF is a multi award-winning inclusive publisher focused on bringing underrepresented voices to the forefront of commercial children's publishing. With a team led by women of colour, and an unwavering focus on their intended readership for each book, Knights Of works to engage with gatekeepers across the industry, including booksellers, teachers and librarians, and supports non-traditional community spaces with events, outreach, marketing and partnerships.